Geraldine Durrant

Pirate Gran
and the Monsters

illustrated by Rose Forshall

NATIONAL
MARITIME
MUSEUM

Gran's very brave.

"When I was young I was the only pirate on board the Black Barnacle who would go to bed with the lights off," says Gran.

All of Gran's old shipmates
are scared of SOMETHING.

BANG

The bosun hates big bangs
and puts his fingers
in his ears when they
fire the cannons.
That's why they call him
Fingers O'Malley.

Flint-Hearted Jack cries in the Crow's Nest because he hates heights.

And when there is
a thunderstorm
Cut-Throat Malone
hides in his hammock
and sucks his thumb.

Even Gran's crocodile worries that crabs will bite his toes...

... in the bath.

But most of all, the pirates are frightened of monsters.

"You're lucky you only have your crocodile underneath your bed," Fingers O'Malley told Gran when the pirates came to stay.

"There's a great big giant thing under my bed with HUGE teeth and SHARP claws and a HORRIBLE long tail."

Gran took out her cutlass and peeped.

"That's not a monster,"
she laughed.
"That's a mouse."

Flint-Hearted Jack was playing hide-and-seek in a dark
cupboard when he felt a hairy gorilla behind him.

"That's not a gorilla," Gran sighed when she rescued him.

"That's my fur coat."

And in the kitchen Cut-Throat Malone jumped
on a chair to escape a giant spider.
"It's green and it's got terrible long legs,"
he told Grandpa.

"It's a tomato stalk,"
said Gran.

When the pirates saw a long, green snake hissing in the garden they were TERRIFIED.

"It was all coiled ready to jump at us," they told Gran.

Gran patted them on the
back and gave them a hug.

"It's not a snake,"
she said.
"It's just Grandpa
watering his flowers."

But when they told Gran they could hear a monster in
the sitting room she was FURIOUS.

"That isn't a dinosaur roaring," she said.

"THAT is a Grandpa snoring."

Gran says it is good to imagine things,
but only if you are writing stories.

"Great big pirates like you should be ashamed of yourselves for being so silly," she said.

So now the pirates don't run away
when they think they see monsters.

They don't hide. And they don't cry.

They just shout "BOO" to make it go away.

And then Gran makes everyone
hot chocolate, and tucks us into
bed with our teddies.

For Patrick, the captain of my ship, my crew mates Eleanor and Alice, and Sebastian the cabin boy.

The first book of Pirate Gran was developed from the winning entry to the
BBC London/RaW 60 second story-writing competition. RaW is the
BBC's biggest ever campaign to help adults across the UK to build
their confidence in reading and writing, by telling stories to their children.

A CIP catalogue record for this book is available from the British Library.

First published in the UK in 2012 by the National Maritime Museum, Greenwich, London SE10 9NF
www.rmg.co.uk

Text © Geraldine Durrant, 2012 and illustrations © Rose Forshall, 2012
Design Simon Davis; project management Kara Green; production management Geoff Barlow
Colour reproduction by Dot Gradations Ltd, UK
Printed in China

ISBN: 978-1-906367-54-1 (hardback)
ISBN: 978-1-906367-55-8 (paperback)

1 3 5 7 9 10 8 6 4 2